Brontosaurus Breath

By Sheila Sweeny Higginson
Based on an episode by Chris Nee
Based on the series created by Chris Nee
Illustrated by Character Building Studio and the Disney Storybook Artists

ABDOPUBLISHING.COM

Reinforced library bound edition published in 2019 by Spotlight, a division of ABDO, PO Box 398166, Minneapolis, Minnesota 55439. Spotlight produces high-quality reinforced library bound editions for schools and libraries. Published by agreement with Disney Press, an imprint of Disney Book Group.

Printed in the United States of America, North Mankato, Minnesota.
042018   092018

DISNEP PRESS
New York • Los Angeles

THIS BOOK CONTAINS
RECYCLED MATERIALS

Library of Congress Control Number: 2017961152

Publisher's Cataloging in Publication Data

Names: Higginson, Sheila Sweeny, author. | Nee, Chris, author. | Character Building Studio; Disney Storybook Art Team, illustrators.
Title: Doc McStuffins: Brontosaurus breath / by Sheila Sweeny Higginson and Chris Nee; illustrated by Character Building Studio and Disney Storybook Art Team.
Description: Minneapolis, MN : Spotlight, 2019 | Series: World of reading level pre-1
Summary: The toys run and hide after Donny "feeds" his toy dino, Bronty. Doc diagnoses Bronty with Stinkysalamibreath. Can Doc fix his stinky breath so the other toys will play with him again?
Identifiers: ISBN 9781532141768 (lib. bdg.)
Subjects: LCSH: Doc McStuffins (Television program)--Juvenile fiction. | Stuffed animals (Toys)--Juvenile fiction. | Personal cleanliness--Juvenile fiction. | Mouth--Care and hygiene--Juvenile fiction. | Readers (Primary)--Juvenile fiction.
Classification: DDC [E]--dc23

Spotlight
A Division of ABDO
abdopublishing.com

Grumble grumble! Roar roar!

That's not the sound of a .

dinosaur

It's tummy growling loudly.
Good thing it's time for lunch!

3

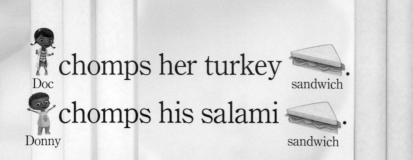

Doc chomps her turkey sandwich.

Donny chomps his salami sandwich.

4

"You look hungry,  Bronty,"  Donny says.
He gives  Bronty a bite of salami.
Then he races off to  soccer practice.

 and her toys are ready.

Doc

It's time to go out and play!

Lambie sees Lenny looking lonely.

She jumps on Bronty's back.

The Dinosaur Delivery Service
is ready to ride.

Their job: cuddles for all!

"Hi, 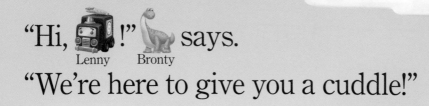!" says.
Lenny Bronty
"We're here to give you a cuddle!"

The  Delivery Service can't

cuddle .

He's racing away from them!

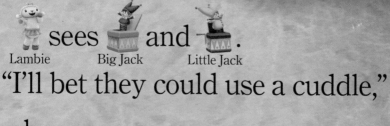

Lambie sees Big Jack and Little Jack.

"I'll bet they could use a cuddle,"

she says.

"Let's go!" Bronty roars.

"Hi, 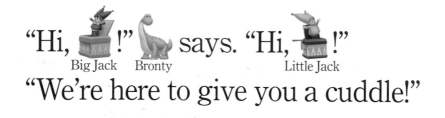!" says. "Hi, ！"

Big Jack   Bronty   Little Jack

"We're here to give you a cuddle!"

The Dinosaur Delivery Service can't
cuddle Big Jack and Little Jack.
They're jumping back into their boxes!

 sees 🐟.

Lambie   Squeakers

"🐟 must want a cuddle," she says.

Squeakers

"Great!" Bronty roars.

"Hi, !" says.

Squeakers   Bronty

"We're here to give you a cuddle!"

The  Delivery Service can't cuddle .

Dinosaur

Squeakers

He's diving under the water!

"Why is everyone running away
from us?" asks .
Lambie
Just then, Stuffy runs up.
"Need . . . hug . . ." he pants.

18

 wants to give her friend
a cuddle.
"Hi, ,"  says. "?"
Oh, no!  passes out!

Lambie

Stuffy   Bronty   Stuffy

Stuffy

"Yikes!" 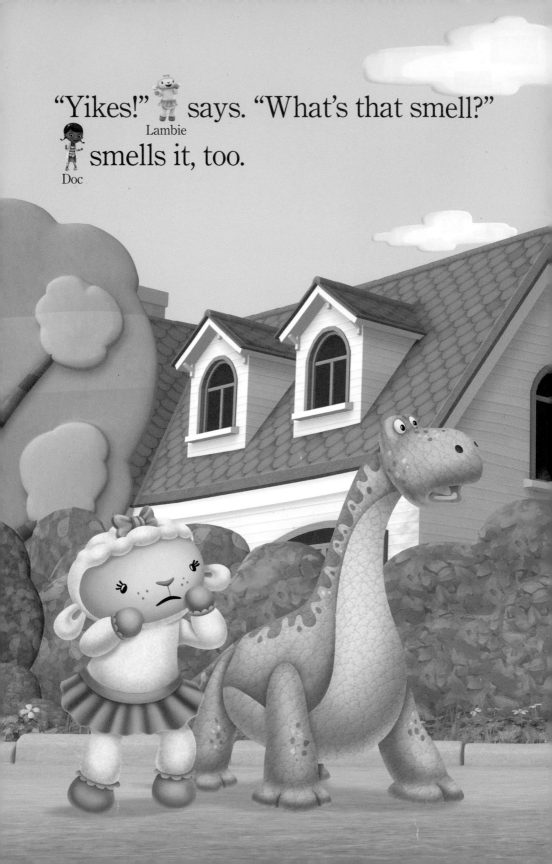 says. "What's that smell?"

Lambie

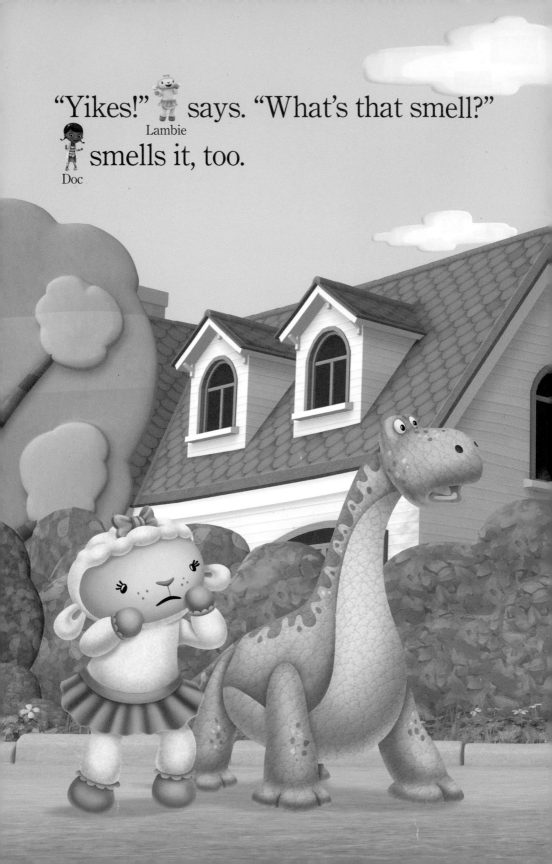 smells it, too.

Doc

It smells like it's time for someone's checkup!

 takes the patient to her clinic. But  patient is not —it's !

Doc

Doc's

Stuffy

Bronty

22

Doc tells Bronty he has bad breath. She needs to check his teeth.

"Open wide," Doc says.

24

 pulls something from  .
Doc   Bronty's mouth

It's a piece of salami!

"You have Stinkysalamibreath,
," says .
Bronty   Doc

"When food gets stuck in your teeth,
it can smell bad," Doc says.

26

[Doc] gives [Bronty] a [toothbrush] and [toothpaste].

She shows him how to brush his [teeth].

"I'm not sticking that thing in my !" says .

mouth   Bronty

 has a great idea.
Lambie
The friends can have a

toothbrushing party!

They can show Bronty that it's fun.

29

🦕 wants to join the party!
Bronty
He brushes his 🦷 with his friends.
teeth
"My 🦷 feel nice and clean,"
teeth
he says.

is all better now.
But will his friends want to play
with again?

Of course they will!